Olivia Hall

Hazel's Christmas Duet

Holiday Haven Novellas #1

ACKNOWLEDGMENTS

I would like to thank my amazing readers for their invaluable feedback: Liz Harmon, Katrina Gullion, Kara Perry, Caroline Stanfield, and Ruby and Gordon Aycock.

Thank you to Lauren Allred for taking the beautiful cover photograph and to Caroline Stanfield for being the gorgeous model.

As always, thank you to my awesome husband for the support, editing, and formatting.

And thank you to my Heavenly Father for the inspiration for this project.

ISBN-13: 978-1981172979
ISBN-10: 1981172971
First paperback edition December 2017

CAVE FALLS PUBLISHING

Contents

For Lauren Rae, one of the bravest people I know.

Chapter 1

HAZEL sat on her couch and watched snowflakes float down past her second-story apartment window. The snow gradually collected on the quaint businesses of downtown Holly Haven, nicknamed "Holiday Haven" by the locals. Colorful Christmas lights and wreaths with red bows lined the streets and doors of the grocery store, movie theater, bakery, restaurant, and bank. Hand-crafted holiday decorations were on display at the school down the road.

Hazel stared across the street at the single wreath on the door of her new place of employment, *Holly Haven Optometrics*. She had begun working as their pediatric optometrist just last week, three weeks before Christmas. Her new boss, Justine, had asked her to decorate the practice, so she hung the wreath. She probably should have done more by hanging some lights too, but she didn't have the desire or motivation to decorate more last week. Maybe she would on Monday.

Hazel stood and walked over to the window. She peered down toward the street and watched as snowflakes continued to fall like dust on the adults grocery shopping and the children building snow forts. She sighed. This little town seemed nice enough, and she didn't have any choice but to leave Minford Village, where she grew up. She frowned. It was all Alden's fault. If he hadn't made their break up so awkward, then it would have been perfectly fine to stay in Minford where she had friends and family. But Alden had been her boss, and they had worked at the only optometrist's office in town. She wanted to start her own practice eventually, but she wasn't financially ready for that yet. What was she supposed to do?

So she had found a new job, a new life. And here she was, alone, in Holly Haven. *Right* before Christmas.

She had tried to convince her parents to spend Christmas with her here. But, of course, they had assumed she would be spending the holidays with

Alden, so they made plans to be in the Bahamas months ago. *Wonderful.*

Hazel knew Alden wasn't right for her. Sure, they had had some fun together, and he had always been enjoyable to be around—until he started acting rude the last couple months. But there was just something missing in the way he had looked at her. She knew his full heart had not been there for her.

And Hazel didn't want half of someone's heart. She wanted the whole, blood-pumping organ.

So, what now? She was stuck in a new town, hours from home, with a new job and no friends. And worst of all, she was alone for Christmas.

Chapter 2

Hazel couldn't stand another minute being alone in her apartment. She texted a couple of her friends in Minford Village to see if they wanted to video chat, but they were all busy. They had moved on with their day-to-day lives without her.

Hazel stood from her couch. It was Saturday afternoon and she had to do *something*.

She put on her hat and gloves and walked outside. She began to pass a charming little bakery that was nestled between the theater and the optometry office and stopped. Golden letters on the window read *Holly's Heavenly Cakes and Custard*.

Hazel pushed a pink cupcake-shaped door open and immediately smelled sweet cream and chocolate. The bakery had the customary glass displays full of fancy desserts. The displays were currently decorated with delicate, paper snowflakes that danced around the edges. Then there were a couple round tables and a few comfy looking floral couches. Amidst the squishy cushions, soft pastel-colored walls, and delicious dessert smells, Hazel felt her mood lift considerably.

"May I help you?" a pretty brunette asked from behind the counter.

Hazel smiled and turned her attention to the glass displays. She hadn't even looked inside yet. "What's good?" She peered closer at some raspberry-filled donuts with stripes of icing on top.

The brunette smiled. "Oh, everything. I have to watch it here." She patted her slim stomach. "I'm Brooke, by the way."

She looked away from the desserts. "Hazel."

"Are you new to Holly Haven?" Brooke said as she brushed some flour off her pink shirt.

Hazel nodded. "Yes, I just got a job next door."

"Oh, at the theater?" Brooke asked, sitting on a stool behind the counter.

Hazel shook her head, motioning to the optometry office. "I'm a pediatric optometrist."

Brooke rested her elbows on the counter. "Wow,

neat. What do you do there?"

Hazel put a piece of pale blonde hair behind her ear. "I work with kids and babies that come in. Give eye exams, that kind of thing."

"Impressive."

"Are you from here?" Hazel asked.

Brooke shook her head. "My sister Sadie and I moved here with our parents about ten years ago. It was my senior year of high school then and now it's Sadie's."

Hazel didn't have a brother or sister but frequently wished she did. "Are you close to your sister?"

Brooke wrinkled her nose. "Most days." She motioned to the display. "So, do you know what you'd like to try?"

Hazel looked down at the plates of cookies, brownies, and muffins. To the right were large tubs of creamy custard. "That vanilla bean custard looks *divine.*"

Brooke nodded. "Good choice. It's one of my favorites. Any toppings?"

Hazel glanced at the different jars of candies, fruit, and baked goods. "Um, cookie dough chunks and strawberries?"

"Sure." Brooke scooped the snowy white custard and put it in a pink polka-dotted bowl before adding the toppings. She passed the bowl to Hazel and then joined her on a couch.

"So, how long have you worked here?" Hazel asked, putting a spoonful of the custard into her mouth and closing her eyes. "Mmm, amazing."

Brooke pulled her long brown hair into a pony-tail. "A year now. My friend Lavanna's family owns the bakery. Her parents wanted her to take over when they retired, but she's not really into baking. Fortunately, I've always wanted to learn how to run a business and I love to bake, so it's a great fit."

"How fun." Hazel twirled her spoon slowly in the thick custard.

Brooke smiled and crossed her legs. "I *love* it."

"That's great."

"So, what brought you to Holly Haven? The new job?"

Hazel hesitated, wondering how much to share about why she left Minford Village. Probably best not to rant about her break-up to her new friend. She took a breath. "Yes, new job, mostly. It was hard moving from my childhood home, but it. . .it was time for a change," she finally said.

"I get it. I hated moving in high school. But I've really grown to love it here. I don't know if I'll ever leave," Brooke admitted.

Hazel put her custard cup on the coffee table in front of the couch. "What makes it so special for you?"

Brooke lifted her shoulders. "I guess I like small towns. The people here are so nice. And of course, I love my friends. Lavanna and Tia. . ."

Hazel's heart ached a little in her chest. She missed her friends in Minford Village. With some of them, it was. . . complicated now. They had been friends with both her and Alden. Now it was like they had to choose. Just like Alden chose to manipulate their friends and make their break-up awkward instead of leaving with grace. Their break-up was like a divorce: their friends were the children, and she was the unwanted parent.

"Any holiday plans?" Brooke asked, breaking the silence.

Hazel shook the depressing thoughts from her head. She looked at Brooke. "Not yet. You?"

CHAPTER TWO

"Mostly just extra time with family and friends. But the bakery is hosting a Christmas party on Christmas Eve. You should come."

Hazel brightened a little as she felt hope spark in her chest. "Thank you, Brooke. I think I will."

Chapter 3

As Hazel began to walk out of *Holly's Heavenly Cakes and Custard*, satisfied from the mouth-watering dessert and good conversation, she noticed a flier on the window. It read "Holly Haven Christmas Orchestra Concert" across the top and "violin and cellists needed" at the bottom.

Hazel peered closer at the silhouette of a woman with her violin and a Christmas tree in the background. "What's this?"

Brooke stood behind her. "Oh, that's the community orchestra's big Christmas event."

Hazel looked closer. "Event?"

"Yes, they donate the proceeds to music programs for the local schools. My friend, Tia, plays the viola," Brooke explained.

Hazel read the flier again. "And they need more

players?"

"They usually do because it's such a big concert. People from surrounding towns even come. Do you play?" Brooke grabbed a broom and began sweeping some crumbs and sprinkles scattered on the wood floor.

Hazel twisted a piece of her hair. "Well, it's been a while. But I play the violin."

"You should go check it out. They meet just down the road past the school. Saturday evenings—I think right now actually. I went to high school with the director; he's really nice." Brooke leaned down to sweep the dust into the pan.

Hazel ripped a small tab off the bottom of the flier that read "Michael Rains, 322 Florence Avenue." "Maybe I will. Thanks, Brooke."

"Bye Hazel. It was really nice meeting you," Brooke said before walking back to the counter.

Hazel stepped outside and turned toward her apartment. Flurries were still floating down from the gray sky, falling on her hat and nose. She turned her head back to the town. Some of the Christmas lights twinkled red, green, and gold. She thought she could hear "Silver Bells" playing faintly from one of the shops.

Hazel glanced again at her lonely apartment building. She didn't want to spend the rest of the evening alone. After last week, not again.

She took a deep breath, turned, and began walking down the main road of town.

A group of teenagers walked toward the theater while a couple kids threw snowballs. A snowball flew through the air and grazed Hazel's ear. Her ear tingled, burning from the icy snow. Hazel grinned. She grabbed some snow and threw it over her shoulder. The snow sprinkled onto the kids like confetti. The kids laughed and threw a couple more snowballs at her as she walked past the elementary school and outside of town.

Hazel looked at the address on the tab and walked into a neighborhood just off the main road. The two-story homes had flickering candles in their windows and evergreen wreaths on their doors. She came to 322 Florence Avenue: a beautiful red brick home with a large tree and rope swing iced over from the snow.

Hazel walked up to the front door and knocked lightly.

CHAPTER THREE

Nothing.

She pressed her ear up to the door, hearing a couple violins playing "This Christmas."

She knocked a little harder and waited. The music stopped. She heard footsteps and the door opened.

Hazel stepped back and a tall lean man opened the door. He was wearing a cardigan and fitted slacks and looked to be in his late twenties or so. He looked past her, over her head, until she made a noise, and then he lowered his head, looking directly at her. Hazel gasped at his crystal blue eyes under his thick reddish-brown hair.

"Hello?" he asked in a soft voice.

Hazel gulped nervously. "Hi, I'm Hazel. I saw your flier. . ."

He nodded, his eyes brightening. "Oh excellent, what do you play?"

"Violin," she said.

"We always need more violinists. Come in."

He stepped back, letting her walk past him. The entryway to the house had glossy wood stairs and floors. The few paintings on the walls and the potted plants on the table made it feel open but not empty.

Hazel followed the man into a large carpeted

room with fifteen or so people and their instruments. He turned toward her again. "This is the crew."

He pointed his finger at the people sitting in the room. "Julian, Margie, Henry, Lily, Matthew, Anna, Tia, Millicent. . ." Hazel nodded and he pointed to seven more people. "And I'm Michael."

Matthew laughed. "How do you do that, Michael? Henry and I are constantly switching seats."

Michael chuckled softly. "*Because* you two are constantly changing seats."

Hazel cocked her head for a moment at Matthew and Henry. Were they twins? She then waved shyly to the group and turned back to Michael. "Would you like me to play something?"

"Sure, if you'd like," he said.

Hazel nodded, finding herself staring at his eyes again. But he didn't seem to mind. He gazed right back at her. She looked away, embarrassed.

Julian turned to her, "You can use my violin, Hazel."

"Thanks," Hazel said, taking the instrument gently in her hands.

She put the violin between her chin and neck and

placed the bow lightly on the strings. She closed her eyes for a moment and then began playing "On My Own" from Les Misérables. Her fingers pressed on the A and E strings as the bow glided back and forth. Fast and then slow. She shifted higher on the E string. Her hand rocked easily as she added vibrato to the tones she played. She got lost in the familiar melody.

When she was finished, Michael was still gazing intently at her, now with small tears in the corners of his blue eyes. "Beautiful—*captivating* performance," he finally said, "Please, join our orchestra."

Chapter 4

HAZEL put some letter charts away as she finished with a patient, a young boy who had been having trouble seeing the chalkboard at school.

Justine, the practice's ophthalmologist and her boss, walked into the exam room as the boy went to the front desk with his mom. "How'd it go?" she asked casually.

Hazel sighed. "Poor kid was *not* happy about getting glasses," she said, sitting in a nearby chair. "I think I got him excited about some frames though. Thick-rimmed and blue. Even I'm a little jealous."

Justine smiled. "Fantastic. I'm glad you're here to pick up some patients. It's a small town, but there actually aren't a lot of optometry offices within twenty-five miles of here."

"So, a lot of patients from neighboring towns?"

Hazel asked, resting her hands in her lap.

Justine nodded, "Exactly."

"Well, I'm glad to be here, Justine. My last work environment wasn't a good. . . fit." Hazel grimaced, thinking about how uncomfortable the last couple of months were working with Alden after he'd dumped her. He had only spoken to her when he had to, and when he did, it was with no feeling, like they had never dated. And, he didn't even bother to make eye contact.

Justine patted Hazel's shoulder, snapping her out of her thoughts. "You can't go wrong with me and Cindy. We're as easy as pie."

Hazel smiled slowly. "I can tell." Cindy greeted her each morning with polite questions about her evening, a cup of steaming hot chocolate topped with whipped cream, and a strawberry scone: the *perfect way* to start the day.

Justine walked across the hall to the file room. Hazel followed behind. "Any fun plans this coming weekend?"

Hazel nodded, stopping by the desk and rearranging a jar of colorful pens. "I'm going ice skating with a girl I met at the bakery and her friends. Then, Saturday, I have orchestra practice."

Justine turned from the file cabinet. "Oh, you joined the orchestra? How nice."

"Yes, it felt great to play. I haven't in a couple years actually." Hazel paused. But, why hadn't she? She had been out of optometry school for a while. She'd had some extra time on her hands. Was it Alden? She vaguely remembered him saying he hated classical music. Yes. . . that must have been it.

Justine combed a stray piece of hair back into her almost-perfect bun. "The orchestra does so well making peoples' hearts light during the holidays. I've been trying to think of something like that to do with the office."

"Like what? Free screenings?" Hazel asked.

Justine began sorting through files. "Maybe. I'll try and think of something."

"Let me know how I can help," Hazel offered.

Justine turned to Hazel. "Thank you. I appreciate that."

"Sure."

As Hazel walked home from work that evening,

she was surprised to see a teenage girl sitting on the curb with a little boy in front of the grocery store. She had rips in her jeans and a beanie on her head. Snow danced around them, clinging to their hats and puffy coats. Their noses and cheeks were rosy, but they looked warm. Next to them was a cardboard box with a sign that read "Free Kittens."

"Hello," Hazel said, stopping near the box and peering in at five fluffy kittens.

"Hi," the girl said, "Interested in a kitten?"

Hazel bit her lip. It was so lonely in the apartment at night. "Maybe. . ."

"Have you had a cat before?" the girl asked.

Hazel adjusted her purse. "Well, sort of. I used to feed a stray that came by back home." She remembered the black cat that she had named Midnight would come by after dinner nearly every night when she was a child. She'd sneak out with scraps while her parents did the dishes because her dad claimed he was "severely allergic to animals of any kind."

"Oh," the girl said. "These are our cat, Sandy's, kittens; they're very sweet. You just need a litter box and food and you're golden." She brought her thumb and pointer finger together to make a circle with her gloved hand.

Hazel laughed, thinking about what it would be like having a kitten on her lap while she read or relaxed on the couch. "I can't believe I'm doing this," she finally said, smiling at the orange kitten pouncing the gray.

"Great! I'm Sadie by the way."

"Sadie?" Hazel paused, "I feel like I've heard that name recently."

Sadie shrugged. "You probably met my sister, Brooke. She works at the bakery."

Hazel nodded. "Yes, yes I have. You're a senior, right?"

"Yes, *thank goodness.* And this is our little brother, Jacob." She pointed at the little boy who had his face cradled in his hands.

"Hi Jacob." Hazel gave a little wave.

The little boy looked at her sadly. "Are you taking our kittens?"

"I—"

"Jacob, I told you. . . Mom said we had to find homes for them," Sadie said, exasperated. "Ongoing battle for the last week," she whispered to Hazel.

Jacob folded his arms and frowned.

Hazel bent down. "If I take a kitten, Jacob, you can bring your sister and come visit."

He sniffed. "Okay."

"So, which one?" Sadie pressed.

Hazel bent down to look closer at the balls of fluff. They were so small that they looked like hamsters. Two black ones were sleeping and a third black kitten was meowing. The orange kitten was playing with a toy mouse while the gray kitten looked curiously at her. When she put her hand down, he rubbed against it and meowed.

"I think the gray," she finally said.

Sadie nodded. "Yeah, he's pretty. In the light he almost looks silver."

Hazel looked over her shoulder. "Well, I guess let me run in and grab some cat stuff at the store and then I'll take him home."

Hazel went into the grocery store and found the pet section. She grabbed a litter box, litter, kitten food, a bowl, a scratch pad, and a couple toys. She paid and went back out.

"Here you go," Sadie placed the soft kitten under one of her arms as she juggled the supplies in the other. "And remember with Christmas coming to avoid tinsel and any string on your tree. Dangerous for cats."

"Well, I don't have a tree, but I'll keep that in mind," Hazel told her.

"Bye Kitty," Jacob said sadly.

Hazel paused. "Hey, Jacob. . . Gee, I wish I had an idea for a good name."

Jacob perked up. "I can help you think of one."

Hazel smiled. "Great! How about something Christmasy?"

Jacob rubbed his chin. "How about Jingle?" he suggested.

"Cute. Maybe I'll buy him a little bell collar," Hazel mused.

"Okay, bye Jingle!" Jacob said as Sadie turned her attention to a little girl pulling her mother's hand and pointing to the box of kittens.

Hazel took the squirmy kitten to her apartment. She put him on the carpet and let him explore a little while she set up his food and water bowls in the kitchen and the litter box in the bathroom. The kitten walked around his food dish for a minute before crawling under her coffee table and through her curtains. She laid some blankets down for a bed and then went to get ready for bed herself.

Feeling tired, Hazel laid down and closed her eyes, but she soon heard meowing on the side of her bed.

She turned to peer at the floor and reached down. "Hey Jingle."

The kitten climbed onto her chest, resembling an oversized gray mouse, and nestled down. He closed his eyes and began purring.

Chapter 5

HAZEL awoke to Jingle curled up right above her head on her pillow. She patted his soft head before getting into the shower.

After she was dressed, she glanced into her cupboards for breakfast. She picked up a box of corn flakes and grimaced. Too bland. She peered out her window at the waking Holly Haven and her eyes rested on the bakery.

She put on her coat, grabbed her purse, and walked straight to the bakery. She was sure Brooke would have something more flavorful for breakfast.

"Hi, Hazel," Brooke said, popping up from behind the counter.

Hazel jumped a little and laughed. "Hey, Brooke. How's your morning?" She glanced at the fresh rows of muffins and cookies.

"Busy, but good. So, I heard you met my little sister and brother. *And* they convinced you to take a kitten."

Hazel laughed. "Yes, they did."

Brooke grinned. "Well, in honor, I made you a special cookie this morning while I made my usual three dozen." She brought out a large cat-shaped sugar cookie with blueish-silver icing from behind the counter.

Hazel's eyes widened slightly. "Wow, you made it for me?" Her friends back home hadn't often gone out of their way for her—not like this, anyway.

Brooke smiled. "It was fun. And it's not every day that you get a new pet."

"It's true," Hazel confessed, "And my dad actually never let me get one. . . I guess I had a goldfish once, but a cat is different."

Brooke put the cookie in a box and passed it over the counter.

"Thanks, Brooke," Hazel said, feeling her heart lighten at Brooke's thoughtfulness.

"Sure."

"Um, could I get something else as well? A muffin maybe?" Hazel asked, her eyes grazing the display windows.

"Oh, I made some cranberry nut muffins this morning," Brooke said.

Her mouth watered. A muffin: just what she needed. "Sounds delicious."

"Great, I'll get you one." Brooke reached into the glass display with a piece of wax paper.

Brooke passed a muffin nearly as big as her face over on a napkin and Hazel gave her two dollars.

"See you tomorrow for skating." Hazel waved as she left.

"Sounds great. Bye Hazel."

Hazel took a big bite of her soft cranberry muffin as she began to walk to work. "Mmm," she said, thinking of the corn flakes and savoring the sweet, tangy taste, "*this* is more like it."

"Sorry?"

Hazel jumped as she looked down at a man sitting on a bench. He had auburn hair, sunglasses, and a cane next to his leg.

She squinted her eyes. "Michael?" she asked.

"Oh, hello. Hazel, right?" Michael said.

"Yes, hi. . ." Embarrassed, she wiped the crumbs from her mouth.

"Sorry, I heard you talking and thought you were talking to me. Anyway, how are you?" he asked, turning his body toward her.

"I'm good, you?" Hazel peered at his sunglasses, wondering what his eyes looked like in the sunlight.

"Fantastic. Just resting on the bench here. I have to go check in on my employees in a minute."

"Where do you work?" she asked.

"I own the movie theater," he replied.

"Oh, I bet you can watch movies all the time. . ." Hazel said, glancing at the list of movies on the front of the theater.

He laughed. "Well, I used to. . . You're an optometrist, right?"

"Yes, I just started here next to the theater."

Michael adjusted his sunglasses. "Justine has always been so kind," he said quietly.

"Yes, I've enjoyed working with her so far. And for her to take me on so quickly. I'm *so* grateful."

"I'm glad it's a good fit."

Hazel glanced over her shoulder at the optometry office. "Much better than my last job."

Michael cocked his head. "How so?"

Hazel shrugged. "Ex-boyfriend who's your boss. . . doesn't work."

Michael nodded. "I get it. Want to talk about it?"

Hazel sighed. "Nah, I won't bore you. Anyway, I'm excited to come to practice this Saturday."

Michael brightened. "I look forward to hearing you play again. I've played for years, but I've never heard anyone play like you. I loved how you took 'On my Own' a couple octaves higher than I usually hear. And playing part of it in the minor key. So melancholy."

"Wow, I, um, haven't picked it up in a couple years actually. I just happened to remember that song."

"Well, I would have never known," he assured her, smiling.

Hazel stared at his puffy hair, even more red in the sunlight. "I better get to work, but nice seeing you, Michael."

"Nice to talk to you as well."

The next day, Hazel ate a quick dinner of a chicken and spinach salad after work and rushed to a little ice rink just outside of town. The rink was already filled with people holding hands and skating as holiday music blasted from a stereo. There was a small hut for skate rentals and another selling cups of hot chocolate and warm donuts.

"Hey, Hazel!" Brooke called from a group of girls. Hazel walked over.

"These are my friends. This is Lavanna," Brooke said, pointing to a girl with bright red hair. "And Tia, and you met Sadie. Girls, this is Hazel. She just moved to Holly Haven."

"Hello!" Lavanna waved.

Sadie sidled up next to her. "How's Jingle?"

"So sweet and cuddly. Did you find homes for the others?"

"All but one black and the orange," Sadie replied.

Brooke motioned to the rental area. "You girls ready?"

Tia held her skates up. "Brought mine."

"Tia could have gone into figure skating," Brooke told her as they walked up to get their skates.

"That's so neat," Hazel commented.

Brooke nodded. "She's very talented. . . at everything. She taught me some spins last year. But I'm certainly out of practice now."

CHAPTER FIVE

"I'll be lucky to stay on my feet," Hazel said as she got some size-eights from the rental booth and found a bench. She took her shoes off and tied the laces tight.

She stood as Brooke, Lavanna, and Sadie clomped their way to the rink like T-rexes. Tia was already gliding gracefully across the ice with her curly black hair bouncing on her shoulders.

Brooke shakily got on the ice and laughed as she began to slip. Brooke quickly grabbed Lavanna, and Lavanna grabbed the wall to stabilize them both. Sadie inched forward behind Brooke.

Tia did a twirl and stopped in front of them. "Here," Tia said, reaching for Brooke's arm. The girls lined up and linked arms, with Tia leading on the far side. Sadie, on the opposite end, held her arm out for Hazel.

"Okay, ladies. Let's take it slow," Tia instructed.

They slowly began gliding across the ice as snow fell onto their noses.

"Hey, we're doing it!" Lavanna shouted.

They picked up the pace, but Sadie stumbled. Suddenly, they were all crashing to the ground. Hazel laughed, despite her wet jeans.

CHAPTER FIVE

They got back up and skated for an hour before huddling with some hot chocolate.

Hazel happily took a sip and listened intently to the other girls' stories and secrets.

She wasn't alone.

Chapter 6

H AZEL sat in the large room of Michael's red brick house. The violinists and cellists tuned their instruments around her. Their sheet music rustled as they turned the pages sitting on the stands.

Hazel studied the sheet music they were practicing, "O Holy Night," one of her favorite Christmas songs. This song always made her feel peaceful, which she needed with so much change in her life recently.

Michael had scheduled for the orchestra to play a couple songs in the lobby of the theater in a few days, but they were all still playing some notes wrong and starting the song too soon or too late.

"All right, let's start from the top," Michael told the group. He started with a thirty second solo before a few violinists began playing. Halfway through the song, Hazel poised her bow on the string as the cellists played a quartet. Hazel's breath caught in her chest as she listened to the enchanting arrangement. The bows moved gracefully across the C, D, G, and A strings. *Beautiful.*

When they were finished, Michael turned to Hazel's chair. "Any chance you'd like to take the solo on page three?"

Hazel studied page three. "Are you sure?"

"Yes," he said, looking past her ear a little.

Michael turned to the rest of the group. "That sounded amazing everyone."

"We messed up like six times," Tia pointed out.

"No one will notice," Michael smiled. "I'm so honored that you're playing my set of arrangements. As you know, I've had a lot of time on my hands in the last few years. And Hazel here," he turned to her, "has just agreed to play the last solo for this piece. Let's practice it with the change and then run through 'Winter Wonderland' and 'White Christmas' one more time."

Hazel put a strand of hair behind her ear. Hopefully she hadn't upset anyone coming in as a new member and already taking a solo. She sneaked a glance around the room. A couple people smiled at her kindly. They didn't look angry.

When the last song was over, Hazel put her violin in its case. She had found it in one of the moving boxes she hadn't yet unpacked. She was glad she had kept it all these years.

She stood to leave and slipped past a few orchestra members who were talking to Michael. He laughed at something one of the girls said. Then he reached out to pat a couple shoulders and shake a few hands.

He had such a calm confidence about him. So different from other men she knew. She'd known cocky men and shy. Generous and selfish. But Michael, he just seemed. . . different.

As she was stuck in her thoughts, his eyes flickered up and she immediately turned beet red. His face was turned in her direction, but he kept talking to the people around him.

She quickly made her way to the front door and out into the falling snow.

Hazel had a few productive days of work before it was the day of the first mini concert at the theater.

She had purposely dressed festively in a red sweater and black jeans that morning. She had spent a good hour before breakfast picking cat hair off her pants as Jingle adorably batted at a toy mouse.

After work, she swung her violin case over her shoulder and went into the bakery for a snack before walking to the theater.

"Hi, Hazel." Brooke smiled as Hazel walked into the bakery. "Want some warm banana bread? Just came out of the oven."

Hazel sat at one of the tables. "Yes, that sounds great. You coming to the concert at the theater?"

Brooke nodded. "Wouldn't miss it. We're closing early tonight and I'm bringing cookies for after the show."

"Oh yum, what kind?" Hazel asked.

"Peanut butter with red and green sprinkles," Brooke said, bringing a large slice of banana bread to her table.

"Mmm, save me one." Hazel took a large bite of the warm bread. "Or, I'll fill up on this. Wow, *so good.*"

"It's my grandma's recipe. It has chocolate chips, walnuts, and cherries," Brooke said while holding up a piece.

Hazel took another bite of the soft, flavorful bread. "What an interesting combination. I love it."

Brooke smiled, cutting her another slice. "How do you like being in the orchestra?"

Hazel swallowed, thinking about the last practice. "Everyone is so nice. It feels great to be playing again. And to just feel appreciated."

"Well, I sure can't wait to hear you and everyone else play. I love Christmas music."

"Me too." Hazel finished her bread and stood. "See you there, thanks for the treat."

Brooke walked her to the door. "Here's a slice for the road. See you soon."

Hazel walked over to the theater and into the main lobby. The theater had red carpets and golden columns and banisters, like a palace. It looked festive all on its own.

Most of the orchestra members were already there, preparing for the show.

Hazel noticed Michael in the corner of the room. Lily and Margie were crying, and Michael was speaking softly and putting his arms around them. After a few minutes, they wiped at their tears and left the theater.

Michael walked over to where everyone was tuning their instruments and putting rosin on their bows. "Lily and Margie have a family emergency and won't be able to play with us tonight."

"What happened?" Henry looked up, frowning.

Michael turned his face in Henry's direction, his blue eyes looking sad.

"Their seven-year-old niece, Emilee, was in a bicycle accident. She's in the ER right now."

Hazel stepped forward. "Will she be okay?"

"They're not sure." Michael said with worry. "So, let's think about them while we play, hope for the best for them and their niece."

The orchestra members nodded and finished setting up. People began to filter into the theater and fill the room. When they were supposed to begin, Michael turned to the audience. "Thank you all for coming. As you know, our series of concerts helps pay for music programs in the local schools. But tonight, we are two players short. Please think about our friends' niece who was just involved in a serious bicycle accident. We hope she will recover very soon."

CHAPTER SIX

He finished speaking and put his violin under his chin. He began playing his solo for "O Holy Night." She watched him sway, passionately putting his heart into the music.

They all positioned and began playing. Hazel kept thinking about the lyrics, "A thrill of hope, a weary world rejoices." The words stirred her soul.

Michael turned toward her when it was time for her solo. His blue eyes looked electric. Her hand shook slightly as she played thinking about the little girl, thinking about her move, thinking about her break-up. Then she looked at Michael and could only think about him.

Chapter 7

HAZEL tried not to stare at Michael at their next practice. Yes, she noticed his bright eyes and ready smile. But she also noticed how he always stopped to listen even if he was busy or stressed. He gave encouragement when needed to his friends and acquaintances.

Her heart leapt whenever she saw him being kind or thoughtful. Her skin tingled when he looked her way. But he didn't always look right at her. Sometimes over her head or past her ear.

She wanted to get to know him better. Learn what he loved, besides music. But was he with someone and just not vocal about it?

Hazel bit her lip as she tried to think and play at the same time. They were practicing a series of new songs for the elementary school performance this Friday: "Frosty the Snowman" and "It's the Most Wonderful Time of the Year." She had to learn both songs from the beginning.

Hazel tried to decide what to do. Try flirting? Ask him out herself? Be honest and say she'd like to get to know him better?

She shook her head at herself. *Snap out of it, Hazel!* She had been calm and collected in her relationship with Alden. Right now, she was acting like a teenager with a big, fat crush.

Wow, she was hooked.

"Hey, Hazel."

Hazel turned behind her. "Hi, Tia."

"What are you doing later?"

Hazel cleared her throat, glancing toward Michael. "Not entirely sure. Why?"

"Lavanna, Brooke, and I wanted to see that new holiday movie at the theater. You should join us."

"Thanks, I might take you up on that." Maybe she'd invite Michael to see it with them.

They played a couple more songs before Hazel began loosening her bow and putting her violin away. She glanced up at Michael who was standing just a few feet from her. He was standing alone.

Hazel took a deep breath and walked up to him.

"Michael?" she asked as she neared him.

He turned his face toward hers and smiled. "Hello, Hazel. Wow, nice alliteration, huh?"

She laughed. "I've actually never gotten that before."

His hand reached out in the air for a moment and then found her arm. Tingles shot up her arm to the back of her neck. "What can I do for you?" he asked.

She took a deep breath. "Um, would you. . . would you like to see a movie tonight. . . with me and some friends?"

He lowered his eyebrows and cleared his throat. "A movie, huh? Um. . ."

Hazel felt confused at his reaction. A movie is totally normal, right? Maybe he thought she was implying something. She turned her face as it colored.

He took his hand off her arm. "A movie with you sounds nice. But. . . I actually have some work to take care of tonight. Thanks for inviting me."

She nodded dumbly. "Of course. See you."

Hazel reddened as she grabbed her coat and walked swiftly into the night.

Hazel pet Jingle while she laid on her couch. She had seen the movie, a romantic comedy, with Brooke, Lavanna, and Tia and then came home.

Hazel turned on her side. She couldn't believe it was two weeks until Christmas. She might still be alone in a lot of ways, but now she had friends and Jingle.

And she had some things to look forward to: the mini concerts and Michael.

Hazel sighed. *Michael.* She wondered if there was another reason he didn't want to see the movie with her earlier. Just then, she felt a buzz from her phone.

"Hello?"

"Hi, dear," a familiar voice said.

Hazel blinked. "Mom? Are you in the Bahamas yet? I didn't expect to hear from you."

"We're not there yet, but on our way. We stopped at some friends for a few days before we left for the cruise."

Hazel stretched her legs. "Oh, having a nice time?"

"Yes, but Hazel, I've called because I've been thinking about you. I'm worried about you."

Hazel took a sip of water from a glass on her side

table. "I'm doing okay, really."

"You lost your boyfriend, job, and friends so quickly. . ." her mother said sadly.

Hazel exhaled. "Mom, Alden and I broke up months ago. And I actually like Holly Haven; it's nice."

"Well, keep me updated, hun." The phone broke out a little. ". . .And go up to Aunt Mimi's for Christmas if you're feeling lonely. She always can plan for one more."

"I'll be okay, really," Hazel reassured her.

"Okay, love you dear. And Merry two-weeks-before Christmas."

"Thanks, Mom, you too. Oh. . ." Hazel paused, ". . .and tell Dad I got a cat."

"A cat? Ha. He'll be thrilled."

"I know."

"Bye, dear."

"Bye." Her parents were officially gone for the season.

Chapter 8

A FTER work Monday, Hazel stopped at the grocery store to get a couple items for dinner. She was looking forward to a relaxing night of tortilla soup and a Christmas movie: Dudley Moore's *The Santa Claus.*

Hazel wanted to get her mind off the awkwardness of Saturday night. She couldn't believe she had just asked Michael out. She really didn't know him. She bit her lip as she carried her bag of groceries out of the store. She did want to get to know him, but maybe he just wasn't interested, even as friends.

She squinted her eyes as dusk had begun to fall on Holly Haven like a gray blanket. She began walking cautiously toward home, as patches of ice had frozen on the ground over the weekend, making the ground look, and feel, like an ice rink.

CHAPTER EIGHT

The streets were nearly empty, except. . .

Hazel narrowed her eyes. Reddish-brown hair flashed in the corner of her eye across the street. Michael?

She looked closer. He had the cane from the other day. . . in front of him. Guiding him?

Hazel froze. *Was she blind?* Was she *totally incompetent* as an optometrist?

Her thoughts continued to race as time seemed to slow down. Hazel saw a car begin to skid at the end of the road. Sliding toward Michael on the ice. She knew now that he could hear the car, but he wouldn't see it.

"Michael!" she screamed as she found her voice. She dropped her groceries and slid across the road to the opposite sidewalk.

He looked up in alarm as she screamed his name again. Luckily, the car was skidding slowly across the ice. Hazel grabbed Michael's arm and pulled him off the sidewalk into the snow as the car hit the sidewalk, bending the front fender.

Michael shook slightly but immediately stood up from where Hazel had thrown him into the snow. "Wha—what happened?"

Hazel stood as well. "A car was sliding on the ice right toward you. I pushed you out of the way. Sorry. . ."

"Hazel? Is that you? You certainly don't need to say sorry. You probably just saved my life or least prevented an injury or two."

"Are you feeling okay? I feel so dumb."

Michael raised his eyebrows. "Why?"

Hazel hesitated. "I didn't realize. . . that you were. . ."

"Blind?" he finished.

"I had no idea."

Michael laughed, softly then loudly.

Hazel reddened and turned her face, even though he couldn't see her.

"I'm. . . sorry," he gasped. "But I'll take that as a compliment."

She stepped forward. "Please do. So many times, you looked right in my direction and just listened so intently."

He scratched his neck. "Well, I can listen just fine. And I'm only partially blind. I can still see. . . colors."

"I—I honestly had no idea. Can I help you home?"

CHAPTER EIGHT

She glanced around for his walking cane. She saw it back where the car had been. The car had left while they were talking. Some people are so thoughtless.

She grabbed the cane and handed it to him. "Or. . ." she began.

Michael cocked his head. "Or what?"

"Um, I was about to make soup and watch a movie. But we could eat dinner and chat. . ."

He smiled, but his eyes slanted down. "I really should get home; I'll make it just fine," he reached out and squeezed her arm, sending a shiver up her neck. "Thank you *so much* for looking out for me."

Hazel watched him leave with her jaw slightly dropped in disbelief and disappointment. He had turned her down again.

Chapter 9

THE next day while Justine and Cindy were taking their lunch break, Hazel began flipping through the patient folders in the front office.

She stopped at "Rains, Michael" and lifted the thick folder from the cabinet. Inside was a small school photo of Michael. He looked maybe sixteen or seventeen. There were several notes about symptoms of wavy vision, blind spots, and blurriness. She flipped to the next page where her eyes focused on the diagnosis: Stargardt disease.

She bit her lip. She wondered how she as an optometrist, didn't recognize someone with macular degeneration. His eyes were so bright and beautiful and kind. She just wasn't thinking clearly.

"That was a sad case."

Hazel snapped her head up, surprised to find Justine behind her.

"Sorry, I didn't mean to startle you."

Hazel put a hand over her racing heart and motioned to the folder. "So, you worked with Michael?"

Justine nodded. "Yes, he came to me for glasses years ago. He had almost perfect vision his whole life, and then suddenly he was having trouble seeing clearly. After coming back several times because the glasses weren't helping, I finally did more research. And, of course, got a background on his family's history."

Hazel glanced back down at the photo of Michael. "I just can't believe that I didn't recognize that he is blind."

Justine sat in a chair. "Well, Michael has lived here his whole life. He knows his way around. And he's always had a certain confidence about him. I don't think that went away with his sight."

Hazel put the folder away. "Well, I think I have an idea, Justine. On what Holly Haven Optometrics can give this holiday season."

Justine raised an eyebrow. "What did you have in mind?"

"Let's raise funds for research on Stargardt disease

and other forms of macular degeneration. I'm sure the other businesses in town would pitch in if we took the initiative to organize an event."

Justine smiled. "I love it."

Chapter 10

H AZEL couldn't help but watch Michael during the next practice and performance. Yes, he did frequently look past people's ears instead of right at their faces, but it was hardly distracting.

Occasionally he would glance up and face her way. She knew that he knew where she sat, but was he really looking in her direction?

"Our niece is doing better," Lily announced as she walked into practice.

Michael brightened. "I'm so glad. How bad was she?"

"Quite a few broken bones, and a concussion. . . she really flew off her bike. But she's responding and everything."

"Is she in the hospital still?" Michael asked.

"Just another day I think."

CHAPTER TEN

"What would she think of an impromptu Christmas concert?"

Lily grinned. "She would *love* that."

Michael clapped his hands together. "Great." He turned to the group. "I've actually already spoken to the activities director at the hospital. She said we're welcome whenever we can make it. So who's up for playing some Christmas carols?"

The group murmured in excitement.

"Great, let's go now then." He paused. "Let's break us all up. A third to the children's side to play for Emilee, then a third to the geriatric side, and the rest of you to the oncology side."

Everyone got up and began putting their instruments away. "Hey Hazel," Tia said from behind her. "Would you like a ride?"

"Sure," Hazel nodded. "Thanks."

They picked up their instrument cases and walked outside to get into Tia's white Camry. Hazel got in the passenger side and buckled her seat belt.

"How far to the hospital?" Hazel asked as Tia started the car.

"About ten minutes," she replied.

Tia pulled off Michael's street and started for the

other side of town.

"How are you liking the orchestra?" Tia asked, turning on the radio.

Hazel put her hands in her lap. "It's wonderful."

"It's great to have you," she said as she tuned into a Christmas station and "Happy Holidays" began playing.

Hazel looked at the twinkling lights as they drove through Holly Haven. "Thanks. Do you perform more than just at Christmas time?"

"We don't play as often other times of the year, but yes. We've done an Easter concert and sometimes we get creative for Halloween too."

"Halloween? Sounds fun."

Tia tapped her wheel. "It is. Michael organized the orchestra five years ago."

Hazel shifted in her seat, glancing at Tia. "How long have you known Michael?"

Tia laughed. "My whole life. We were in the same elementary class four years in a row." She made a turn.

"Oh, so before. . ."

Tia nodded. "Yes, it's really heartbreaking. He was super athletic. Played varsity for all our major high school sports. Soccer, baseball, tennis. It started getting worse senior year. He could still play, but it wasn't the same."

"That's horrible."

Tia sighed. "That's not even the worst of it."

Hazel raised her eyebrows. "Really? What else?"

"Marilee, his girlfriend of three years, left him when it began to get really bad. She claimed she didn't have feelings anymore. . . but I heard her more than once talk about 'Michael's new handicap.' "

"That's so mean."

Tia shrugged. "She wasn't a mean person really. Just immature and scared. She didn't deserve him."

"Has he dated since?"

Tia turned slightly and raised an eyebrow. "Why, interested?"

Hazel blushed. "Michael isn't like anyone I've ever met."

"Sounds like you have a crush."

Hazel bit her lip. "Yes, I guess a little."

Tia sighed. "He hasn't dated *seriously* since he became blind. Since Marilee. I'd love to see him in love again."

"Did he love her?"

Tia nodded. "The tragedy is, I think he did."

They pulled into the hospital.

Hazel stopped Tia as she turned to get out of the car. "Don't tell him what I said."

Tia flipped her hair over her shoulder. "Don't worry, I wouldn't do that. But Hazel, don't be afraid to tell him how you feel."

"Well, I kind of got rejected by him. Twice."

"Just be open with him. Let him know you're not playing games." Tia grabbed her viola and got out of the car.

Hazel walked around the car to Tia. "And if that doesn't work?"

Tia shrugged. "Try as hard as your heart can take. And just move on if he doesn't seem interested."

Hazel bit her lip. "It's hard to put my heart out there like that."

Tia put her hand on Hazel's shoulder. "But you'll never know if you don't try."

Ten minutes later, Hazel was setting up her violin on the children's side. Michael, Margie, Lily, and

Anna were getting their violins out as well.

Margie pointed to a room down the hall. "Emilee is just down here. She'll be so surprised."

They walked into a room with a small girl on the hospital bed. She had an arm and leg cast and bruises on her exposed arm and face. Some balloons and cards were lined up on her windowsill.

"Aunt Margie and Lily?" the little girl said, perking up.

"Hey Emilee, we brought some friends."

She smiled, looking at their instruments. "Are you going to play music for me?"

Michael smiled back. "What's your favorite Christmas song, Emilee?"

"Jingle Bells," she said without hesitation.

"All right!" he turned to the players. "Who all knows it?"

Hazel reddened. She'd been playing it for her cat. "Um, I can play it."

Michael nodded. "Okay, let's start together with the intro, and whoever can join in with staccatos for the chorus."

Hazel stood by Michael and they began playing in sync. Her heart beat wildly to the music they created with their duet. Michael was the talented one. With the chorus, Lily and Anna jumped in, playing enthusiastically beside them. By the end, Emilee was clapping excitedly. "Again!"

Michael turned to her and smiled, his eyes bright like Christmas lights. "You ready?" he whispered.

"Yes," she said, breathlessly.

Hazel got into her pajamas later that night and sat on her couch with a bowl of popcorn. She reflected on the evening. The snowflakes had been like mini marshmallows falling from the sky as they walked out of the hospital. She even craned her face up to catch a few on her tongue. They all had felt so light making the patients happy. The beautiful snow just added to their good mood. It took all of Hazel's willpower to not give Michael a hug at the end.

Jingle came and sat at her feet. She rubbed his chin and thought about what Tia had said. Maybe she should just put herself out there more. And if he's not interested, try and forget him. But would he just keep rejecting her?

She sighed. He was special for sure. But she didn't

need another dramatic relationship after what she had been through with Alden.

But seeing if something could be there was worth it. . . right?

Chapter 11

T HE next evening, Hazel joined Brooke, Lavanna, Tia, and Sadie at the bakery for cookie decorating. Brooke had made dozens of bell, reindeer, snowflake, and star-shaped sugar cookies and laid out red, blue, yellow, and green frosting and butter knives. "White Christmas" played merrily from the stereo.

"This is my favorite tradition," Sadie said, licking some blue frosting off her finger.

Brooke laughed. "Don't forget to make a plate for our neighbors."

"And some for the nursing home," Tia added.

"I have a date with a plate of cookies later tonight," Lavanna said, taking a bite and closing her eyes. "Seriously, Brooke, you make the best frosting."

Hazel laid out three paper plates, putting six cookies on each. She planned on keeping a plate for herself, giving one to her neighbor, and bringing a plate to Michael.

"How's school, Sadie?" Tia asked.

Sadie put her hand on her face. "Ugh, the worst. I cannot wait to graduate."

"Just a few more months," Brooke said encouragingly. "Besides, you have your music to get you through."

"What do you play?" Hazel asked.

Sadie took a bite of a cookie she was frosting. "Guitar. I try to write songs."

"And they're awesome," Brooke added.

"Michael could actually use a guitarist for some of the songs he writes for the orchestra," Tia said.

Hazel stopped. "Wow, that would be amazing to hear. Michael's other songs are so beautiful."

Lavanna lifted an eyebrow and smiled. "Do you like him, Hazel?"

Hazel blushed. "Maybe."

Lavanna nodded. "I can see you two together. It just. . . works."

"You really think so?"

"I do."

Hazel's heart flipped. She hoped so.

The next morning, after the elementary school concert, the kids clamored up to them to shake the players' hands and poke at their instruments. Finally, their teachers ushered them away.

From "Rudolph the Red-Nosed Reindeer" to "Light One Candle," the kids had happily sat and sung along. They were now eating holiday cookies and sipping juice that Matthew and Millicent had brought.

Michael put his violin away and stood with his walking cane poised under his arm like a baton.

Hazel was still putting her violin away when he walked up behind her. "Hello."

She stood. "Michael, hi. . ."

"Beautiful playing this performance. I could hear you to my left."

"Thank you."

He cleared his throat. "I wanted to apologize for not staying for dinner the other night, especially after you saved me."

"You didn't have to, just because of that—"

Michael reached out slowly until he touched a piece of her hair. And then let his hand drop. "It would have been nice. But best not to. . . get too close," he finished.

Hazel frowned. "Why? You can trust me."

He raised an eyebrow. "I don't know you."

She stepped forward. "You could try," she said quietly.

His normally bright blue eyes looked shadowed. "Believe me, I'd like to." He pulled his cane out in front of him and found his way over to the refreshment table.

Hazel sighed. *How could she convince him?*

She walked up beside him while he got a cookie. "Michael?"

"Yes, Hazel?"

"Just hear me out."

He took a bite and chewed. "Okay."

"I just left. . . a failed relationship. The feelings were reciprocated for a time. But. . . there was something missing. It just wasn't all there, ya know?"

He nodded.

"But, I feel drawn to you. . . I don't know how

to explain it, but I feel like it's worth giving you and me a chance."

"Hazel. . . I'm blind."

She touched his arm softly. "It's okay."

He sighed, his blue eyes troubled. "It will. . . matter to you."

"Michael—"

He hesitated, turning to her. "Let's just go out as friends. First. And then, maybe. . ."

She nodded slowly. "Okay."

"Okay. Friday night?" Michael asked.

"Yes."

Chapter 12

HAZEL watched Justine lead a patient to Cindy in the front before joining her in the file room.

"Have you thought any more about what to do for the fundraiser?" Justine asked, putting a file on the shelf.

Hazel nodded. "Yes, actually. I'm thinking a kid's carnival. I could get some friends from the orchestra to volunteer and local businesses to donate."

"Sounds fun."

Hazel opened a blueberry granola bar. "We can have games, prizes, an auction, and maybe live music." She took a bite.

"Would this take away from the orchestra's efforts to raise money for music programs?"

Hazel threw the wrapper away. "Hmm. . . well, we could do it the week before New Year's, after the concert, to be safe."

Justine smiled. "Nice thinking, Hazel."

"I could get started after work and see which businesses want to participate."

"Perfect; you're the best."

Later that day, Hazel walked over to *Holly's Heavenly Cakes and Custard.* Brooke stood from a stool when she walked in.

"Hey, girl. What can I get for you?"

Hazel brought out an information sheet. "I'm actually here to see if the bakery would be interested in participating in a fundraiser my office is putting together."

"Of course! What's it for?"

Hazel put a piece of hair behind her ear. "Research for macular degeneration."

Brooke grinned. "For Michael?"

Hazel reddened. "Well, I had him in mind."

"Well, I'm glad you like him. He's a great guy," Brooke commented. "But be careful. He certainly has. . . trust issues."

"Can you blame him?"

Brooke shook her head. "No, I can't." She tapped the counter. "Anyway, of course we'll participate. I'll make six dozen cookies to sell and a couple cakes and pies. Any special kind of theme for the event?"

Hazel glanced outside. "Just winter."

"Okay, maybe some snowflake sugar cookies and a coconut cake." Brooke clasped her hands excitedly. "Ooh, and maybe I'll decorate something in the shape of an eye."

Hazel laughed. "I love it."

Brooke reached behind the counter and brought out chocolate squares with red swirls. "Try this chocolate peppermint fudge. It's delicious." She put a piece on a small plate and passed it over the counter.

Hazel put a square of the creamy fudge into her mouth. The fudge melted onto her tongue like ice cream. "Wow, *mmm*. I'll take a slice of that."

"You got it."

As Hazel turned to leave with her fudge, Brooke stepped out from behind the counter. "Oh, Hazel?"

"Yes?"

"Try not and get your heart broken. Tia and I have been friends with Michael for years and we've seen him struggle with being loved. . . in that way."

CHAPTER TWELVE

"I understand. But I *really* want to try anyway," Hazel said.

"I'm glad. That might make the difference."

Chapter 13

WITH a week until Christmas, Hazel caved and bought a small tree at a drugstore right outside of Holly Haven. She put it on a small table near her window out of Jingle's reach, even though he had been jumping higher and higher lately.

Jingle watched her curiously as she decorated the small tree. "Now, for you," she pulled a big box out of a shopping bag. "You can think of this as an early Christmas present."

Her kitten rubbed against her leg as she opened the box and pulled out several pieces to a kitty scratch-pad and gym. It had a base with a post to scratch and a perch on the top. A toy mouse and ball dangled from the top.

She assembled the pieces. Jingle rubbed his head on the base before scratching the post and jumping on the perch. He then laid on the perch and batted at the mouse.

She rubbed his head. "Glad you like it."

Hazel was happy to have a pet and friends. She couldn't believe that just two weeks ago she was completely alone. Now, she had a date with Michael to look forward to.

She glanced at the clock. She had an hour before she'd meet him at the movie theater. She wondered what he had planned since he didn't "watch" movies anymore.

Hazel put on a stretchy floral shirt with some comfy jeans. She then applied a little blush and some mauve lipstick. She let her blonde hair fall around her face.

Interesting. Michael probably doesn't know the color of her hair or eyes. Or what she looks like at all. He only knows her voice and her music.

She wondered if he'd ever ask to feel her face like she'd seen in movies. . . She turned as pink as raspberry rose soufflé at the thought.

Once she was ready, she said goodbye to Jingle and walked out of her apartment. She glanced up at the old-fashioned headboard of the theater and saw they were playing a rerun of "Holiday Inn." How fun.

Hazel walked into the lobby where groups of people were buying tickets or popcorn made from an old-fashioned popper. The popcorn kernels popped merrily to some classical Christmas music.

Hazel saw Michael up the stairs near the entrance to the main theater room. He wore a button-up blue shirt, matching his eyes, and khaki slacks. His copper-colored hair was styled with a flip in the front. He didn't have his cane.

She walked slowly up the stairs to him. "Hi."

He smiled. "Hi."

He offered her his arm. "Shall we?"

She took his arm, feeling her heart skip a beat. "Sure."

Instead of taking her into the theater, he led her to the stairs. She held onto his lean but muscled arm as he led her to a room at the top of the stairs. He opened the door, and she saw lots of buttons and the projector. Next to the projector were two chairs, a small table, and a large bowl of popcorn.

Michael led her to the chairs. "I thought we could talk while I start the movie."

She sat and popped a piece of buttery popcorn

into her mouth. "Sounds fun."

He took a few minutes to press some buttons and get the movie started. Soon, they could see *Holiday Inn* begin through a glass window to the main theater room. Then he sat in a chair next to her. "So, where are you from?"

Hazel crossed her legs. "A town a few hours from here. Minford Village. Have you heard of it?"

He took a piece of popcorn. "Maybe once or twice. Do you miss it?"

"The people, yes. But I am enjoying it here in Holly Haven so far," she said.

"Even coming by yourself?"

"I admit, it was hard at first. But I've made some friends. And I got a cat."

"A cat, huh? Pets can help with loneliness."

Hazel cocked her head. "Do you have a pet, Michael?"

He shrugged. "I did. A dog. But he died a couple years ago."

"I'm sorry."

Michael pressed his lips together. "Thanks, Hazel." He leaned back in his chair. "How long have you played the violin?"

Hazel looked down. "Through middle school and high school, but I hadn't picked it up in a couple years before moving here."

"Why?"

She fiddled with her hands. "I cared too much about what my ex thought of me. I guess it seemed like a waste of time to him."

"Do you still care?"

"Not at all," she said, knowing it was true. "How about you? How long have you played?" She chewed on a piece of popcorn.

He sat back in his chair. "I played as a child and stopped as I grew older. I got back into it when this. . ." he motioned to his eyes, "happened."

"I see."

He laughed. "Yes, you do."

She put her palm on her face. "Sorry."

He shook his head. "No, don't apologize. It's true. You can see, but I cannot."

She looked at his profile. "What's your world like?"

Michael hesitated and turned to face her. "Blurred colors, dark. But music and making people happy help bring some light back."

CHAPTER THIRTEEN

She put her hand on his gently. "I'm glad."

He accepted her hand, his expression holding a glimmer of hope. "Me too."

Chapter 14

Three days later, Michael invited Hazel to his house for dinner. He made Tuscan soup and they played an adapted version of Scrabble. She didn't know there was such a thing.

Hazel put her hand near Michael's and he ran his slender finger up and down her knuckles. "When did you start working at the movie theater?" she asked.

"As a teenager. My uncle owned the theater then and offered me an after-school job." Michael arranged his tiles, feeling their raised bumps as he went.

"Did you like it?"

Michael paused. "As a child, I thought the theater was magical. I forgot that a little when I began working there as a janitor at age fifteen." Michael put his hand under his chin. "But soon, I remembered that feeling and knew that working at the theater was the perfect job for me. I got a degree in business and bought the theater when my uncle retired."

"Well, it's beautiful."

Michael's mouth turned down for a second before nodding. "Yes, it is. I remember that too."

Hazel looked down. "I'm sorry to keep reminding you. . ."

He took her hand. "It's not you; so many things remind me of my world before. . . But just listening to the sounds of the theater makes me happy."

"Is it hard to remember?"

He squeezed her hand. *"Incredibly."*

After their game, they sat close on Michael's couch and listened to Nat King Cole's *The Magic of Christmas* album.

The next night, they walked along the sidewalk in front of the shops in town. Christmas music floated above their heads, serenading them.

Michael took Hazel's hand. "Do you have a favorite Christmas memory?"

She turned slightly. "I think the Christmas that my family and I got snowed in."

CHAPTER FOURTEEN

"Really?"

Hazel smiled. "Yes. My parents and I just got in comfy clothes, drank hot chocolate, and read Christmas romances. It was a beautiful holiday."

He played with a piece of her silky hair. "That does sound dreamy."

They stopped in the bakery and shared an apple turnover before Michael took her home. He wrapped his arms around her, holding her close to his chest and then left.

By Thursday, the night before Christmas Eve, Michael had declined Hazel's offer to make Christmas cookies. The next morning, he didn't text back at all.

Finally, worried, she texted asking if he was okay. He responded with "yes." *Ugh.* The one-word texts. Alden was a fan of those. . .

Hazel hoped he'd be coming to the bakery's Christmas Eve party that night. But she couldn't remember if he said he had plans. At least she'd see him at the Christmas concert the next day.

She sighed and spent the day baking cookies and

reading a Christmas novel with Jingle on her lap.

An hour before the party, she put on her sweater, lipstick, and some seasonal holly leaf earrings. She smiled, feeling a little like a Christmas tree, and put on her coat. She walked out of her apartment building and down the road to the bakery.

Hazel walked inside the bakery and inhaled gingerbread and vanilla. The front counter and tables were covered in red and green bows and sparkly stars made of paper. "Let it Snow" played from a stereo. People from town mingled holding their plates filled with spinach artichoke dip, homemade tortilla chips, quiche, fruit, and an assortment of cookies.

Hazel licked her lips as Brooke approached her with a Christmas tree plate full of caramel marshmallow truffles. "This looks great, Brooke." She put a gooey truffle into her mouth.

Brooke smiled happily. "Thanks, we are having a nice turn-out."

Lavanna and Tia walked up next to Brooke. "Hi, Hazel," Lavanna said.

"Hi, good to see you all." Hazel turned to the table to fill her plate with the dip, chips, pineapple, and two snickerdoodles.

CHAPTER FOURTEEN

"I've heard you've been busy," Lavanna teased.

Hazel looked away. "Oh Michael? Yes, we've had some nice dates. He's been quieter the last day or so though."

"Typical Michael," Tia said with a frown.

Hazel turned. "Really?"

Brooke nodded sadly. "He'll go out with a girl he likes a couple times. And then, before he gets too close, he stops responding."

Hazel put her plate down in frustration. "Well, I'm not giving up that easily."

Brooke touched Hazel's shoulder. "What are you going to do?"

"Not sure. I have to do something."

Lavanna nudged her. "Well, here's your chance."

Hazel turned as the door opened with a flurry of snow and Michael walked into the bakery.

Chapter 15

H<small>AZEL</small> took a deep breath and met Michael at the counter. "Hi, Michael."

Michael jumped slightly. "Hello Hazel."

"Here for the party?" she asked casually.

He cleared his throat. "No, actually. I'm checking with Brooke on the dessert order for the concert tomorrow."

"Oh."

He turned his face away. "Sorry, um, that I couldn't come yesterday."

"Me too."

He looked sad for a moment but cleared his throat. "Is Brooke around?"

She turned. "Yeah, I'll get her."

Hazel walked up to Brooke, who was still talking to Tia and Lavanna.

CHAPTER FIFTEEN

"Did you tell him off?" Lavanna asked.

Hazel's shoulders dropped. "Oh, that was never the plan. I can tell he seems sad though."

Tia glanced over her shoulder. "I think you're right. Poor guy."

"He's asking for you, Brooke."

Brooke sighed. "All right."

Brooke went to Michael and took a sheet of paper from him. She nodded a few times before he left.

Brooke walked back and put her arm around Hazel's shoulders. "He's missing out." She then turned to the party. "Who's ready for my favorite game, Psychiatrist? Let's put some chairs in a circle."

After the party, Hazel went back to her apartment. Her new friends were all busy with their families for the rest of Christmas Eve.

She decided to pop *Elf* in and cuddle with Jingle on the couch. Her little Christmas tree sparkled in the window. She sighed and fell asleep before the movie was over.

Chapter 16

THE next morning, Hazel stretched on her couch. Jingle was purring by her feet.

She blinked at her little tree and the freshly fallen snow in the town behind it. It was Christmas morning.

She went to her kitchen for a glass of milk and jumped when the doorbell rang.

She opened the door to find a large package addressed to her from her parents—they must have asked a friend to mail it before they left—and a plate of cinnamon rolls. She touched a cinnamon roll through the plastic, still warm, and noticed a note from Brooke under the plate.

Hazel put a large cinnamon roll on a plate and took a gooey bite. She licked her lips; it was *scrumptious*. She took her package to her living room to open it by a tree.

One by one, she pulled out a book from her favorite author, a Blu-ray copy of *The Phantom of the Opera,* a lotion kit, a box of chocolates, a homemade scarf, and a framed picture that said, "It's A Wonderful Life," her parent's favorite movie. She smiled at their thoughtful gifts and wished they were with her.

She got dressed and put her scarf on before going down to the restaurant for lunch. She ordered creamy crab soup and a cranberry kale salad.

After lunch, she listened to Christmas music lazily on her couch and dangled a toy for Jingle before getting ready for the concert.

She put on an ivory dress and let her curled hair fall around her shoulders. Her heart pounded in her chest like a thunderstorm at the thought of seeing Michael.

Hazel took her violin and walked to a local church, where the concert was being held. It was a stone church just past Michael's house and the ice rink.

She walked through the large doors leading to a high-ceiling room with tall windows on the sides. Rows and rows of pews led to a stage in the front.

People were already beginning to file in.

Hazel saw Michael at the front, tuning his violin. He wore a gray suit with a vest and a blue tie. He looked stunning.

"Hi, Michael."

He smiled kindly, all the stiffness from the previous night gone.

"Hello, Hazel. Merry Christmas."

"Merry Christmas. I like your suit."

He reached over and touched her sleeve on her shoulder and rubbed the satin for a moment. "Well, your dress feels nice. I'm sure it's beautiful." He turned back to his violin.

She shivered and rubbed her arms. "Thanks. Are you excited for the concert?"

His eyes shone. "My favorite night of the year."

She smiled, feeling his enthusiasm and got her own instrument out.

Michael walked up behind her. "Are you ready for our duet in 'Have Yourself a Merry Little Christmas'?"

"Yes."

He smiled. "Perfect. I love performing with you."

She blinked, taken aback by his forwardness after how he had acted the night before.

"Are you okay, Michael?"

He sighed. "Hopefully someday I will be."

At six p.m., the lights dimmed and a hush fell over the people packed in the pews. Even the small babies and children looked forward curiously.

Michael stepped forward. "Thank you all for coming out for our concert. Welcome back if you've been before and we're glad to have you if it's your first time. We're going to play seven pieces for you and will invite you to sing along for the last song. Enjoy and Merry Christmas."

Michael began with an unaccompanied "Silent Night." The room was still. Hazel glanced at the beautiful stain glass of Jesus behind them and realized it couldn't be more perfect. The group then played "The First Noel" with Tia doing a solo in the middle. Hazel could see a couple in the front row dabbing their eyes with tissues. They played "I Heard the Bells on Christmas Day" and "Joy to the World." A child sleeping on his father's shoulder awoke and stared at them in wonder. The group played "Winter Wonderland" with a special cello part. Then "The Christmas Song."

Finally, Michael and Hazel stepped forward for their duet of "Have Yourself a Merry Little Christmas."

Hazel's heart felt light as she played next to Michael. He played passionately next to her.

When the audience began to sing the third verse, she noticed he slowed down a little. At the words "Through the years, we'll all be together," his eyes glistened. When they finished, he wiped at his eyes and stepped forward.

"Thank you all *so much* again for being here. All proceeds from this concert go to music programs for the elementary school. Drop any donations off near the dessert table in the back. Merry Christmas and Happy New Year, Holiday Haven and friends!"

The crowd cheered and began to get out of their seats.

Hazel saw Michael walk back toward her. "Hazel, I. . .," he put his hand on the silk of her dress again.

"Yes?"

He pressed his eyebrows together and paused.

Finally, he simply said, "Merry Christmas," before walking away.

"Merry Christmas, Michael," she whispered after him.

Chapter 17

THE week between Christmas and New Year's, Hazel put her energy into distracting herself from Michael and preparing for the Stargardt fundraiser.

She sighed as she decorated the school gym with Justine, Cindy, Tia, Lavanna, Brooke, and Sadie. She knew she and Michael had something special, different from what she had felt for Alden. She knew Michael saw her for her, not just for her talents. She knew their relationship had potential, but she wasn't sure what to do about it.

"Beautiful Christmas concert," Sadie said beside her as she put lights around the front booth.

"Thanks, Sadie."

Sadie arranged some name tags. "I loved your duet at the end. It was amazing."

"It seemed like Michael got a little emotional," Lavanna said, coming to help with the lights.

Hazel nodded. "Yes, and I'm not totally sure why."

"He likes you," Tia said.

Hazel stopped. "How are you so sure?"

"His body language toward you. And he turns his head in your direction so attentively."

Hazel sighed, looking at the lights. "Well, I definitely care for him."

"He hasn't acted this way toward a girl since Marilee. I guess be patient with him, Hazel."

The group set up the games for the kids and the donated gifts for the silent auction. They arranged a large craft table and a dessert table. Lavanna volunteered to make balloon animals while Tia and Brooke face painted. The place was covered in lights and homemade decorations from the third and fourth graders.

Sadie had volunteered to play the guitar and sing with a couple other friends. She tuned her guitar and began playing "What Are You Doing New Year's

Eve?"

Around one p.m., kids began filing in with their parents. They clamored for the games, face painting, and balloon animals while their parents wrote down their bids for the gift baskets.

Halfway through, Hazel was surprised to feel a tap on her shoulder. She turned to see Michael. His eyes were large and glistening.

"Michael, hi—"

Michael took her hand. "I just heard—I just wanted to say you're amazing to do this. To raise funds for Stargardt's," his voice broke.

She stepped forward. "Of course, I wanted to. People should understand it better."

He tentatively stepped forward and reached for her. As he began to wrap his arms around her, she heard her name from across the gym, spoken by a familiar voice, a *very familiar voice.*

She gasped as she turned around. *Alden.*

Chapter 18

Hazel cleared her throat. "Michael? Would you excuse me for a moment?"

"Sure, are you okay?"

"Yes," she nodded. "I just need to take care of something."

Hazel walked away from Michael to Alden who was waiting for her by the dessert table, sampling a snowflake cookie.

"Alden?"

"Hazel! I've missed you!" Alden said, turning and pulling her into a hug.

Hazel pulled away. "Alden, what you are doing here? How did you know where to find me?"

He shrugged. "There's hardly anyone on your main street right now. I just followed the noise here and saw you."

CHAPTER EIGHTEEN

"What are you doing *here* though?" she repeated.

Alden took her hand. "Christmas was lonely without you. I decided I didn't want to spend New Year's away from you as well. Thought I'd surprise you."

Hazel took a breath. "Alden, you need to know. . . I'm seeing someone now."

Alden raised an eyebrow. "But you've only been gone for three weeks."

"I know."

Alden stepped forward, touching her arm. "C'mon, Hazel. What do you say? I can stay up here for a few days till New Year's and then we can talk about going forward after that. I made a *huge* mistake."

Hazel shook her head. "Alden, I'm sorry, I know you came a long way to see me. But you need to know that it's over between us. I don't have feelings for you, and I'm not sure if I ever did."

"Hazel. . ."

Michael walked up and put his hand on her arm. "Hazel? Are you okay?" he asked.

Alden frowned. "Who's this?"

"This is Michael, who I was telling you about.

We're dating."

Alden scrunched his face as he studied Michael. Suddenly, he turned and whispered to Hazel, "*Wait*, is he blind?"

Hazel glanced at Michael and smiled. "*Yes*, Alden. He is."

"Uh, hi Michael." Alden waved awkwardly before turning to Hazel. "Can I talk to you for a minute? Alone?" He pulled Hazel a few feet away.

"*What*, Alden?" Hazel said.

Alden folded his arms across his chest. "Are you serious about this guy?"

Hazel nodded. "It's only been a couple weeks, but I really want to see where this goes."

"But Hazel. . . You might not care now, but down the road. . . You'd have a *completely* different life. No more skiing or road biking—"

Hazel rolled her eyes, beginning to feel angry. "Those were all things you liked, Alden."

"I bet he can't even drive."

Hazel shook her head. "*Stop.* I'm sorry, Alden. I did care for you, but what I felt for you isn't what I feel for Michael. Michael is important to me. To who I am—who I'm becoming."

CHAPTER EIGHTEEN

"Huh?"

Hazel squeezed Michael's hand as he came to stand beside her. "He reintroduced music. And he's such a *kind* person. And the way he looks at me. . ."

Alden rolled his eyes. "He can't even *see*, Hazel."

She turned to Michael, ignoring Alden. "He sees me more than you ever did."

"Whatever. I guess you have poorer judgment than I thought," Alden snapped.

Hazel rubbed the bridge of her nose. "Please, just leave, Alden."

"Fine," he said, turning and storming out of the gym.

Hazel turned to Michael in relief.

"So that was Alden?"

Hazel put her hand on her face. "Uh, yes. . . I hope you didn't hear all that. I've really learned the last couple months that he can be a real jerk."

Michael stepped in front of her. "I did hear actually. . . one of the few perks of losing my sight I guess. Anyway, I was more interested in what you had to say. Do you mean all that, Hazel?" He touched her hair in wonder.

"Mean what?"

He cocked his head. "That, despite my. . . situation, despite what us being together would mean down the road, you're still willing to take the chance."

"I didn't actually say those words—"

Michael stepped closer. "I heard it in your voice."

She smiled slowly. "Yes, Michael. . ."

He carefully touched her forehead, eyes, nose, and lips, before kissing her softly. Then firmly.

He pulled away but kept his face near hers. "Do you have plans New Years Eve?" he whispered.

She looked up at his bright eyes before kissing him back.

— A few days later —

Michael and Hazel sat on Hazel's couch watching the glittery snow fall outside the window. Hazel's little Christmas tree's lights twinkled. Jingle crawled across their laps along with the black kitten that Hazel had gotten Michael as a late Christmas present.

Hazel watched her phone clock turn from 11:59 to midnight. "It's a new year," Hazel said, squeezing

CHAPTER EIGHTEEN

Michael's hand.

Michael pulled her closer, his lips grazing her cheek. "Yes, it is."

About the Author   Olivia Rian was born and raised in Ohio, where she experienced her first kiss, first love (buckeye chocolates), first relationship, first break-up, and first (and only!) honeymoon. After surviving a few frosty winters in the Mountain West, she received a degree in English from Brigham Young University–Idaho. She now lives in the DC metropolitan area, closer to her original home in the Midwest. Olivia enjoys reading a good romance, shopping, biking, baking dessert (no surprise to her readers), and making trips to the beach with her husband and two kids.

Made in the USA
San Bernardino, CA
28 November 2017